The Prince's Matchmaker

Cowboy Fairytales: The Next Generation

Lacy Williams

Chapter One

"Your mother is worried about you."

Valentin, crown prince of Glorvaird, looked up from the newspaper headline that had captured his attention.

His father, Cody Austin, strode into the blue breakfast room with his usual loose-limbed cowboy swagger. Valentin had attempted to imitate it once. He'd been all of ten, and his mother had politely hinted that a future king couldn't walk like that.

Mother's hints were always polite. Until they weren't.

"I'm fine," Valentin told his father as the older man settled in the chair across the small, round table covered in white linen and fine china. He folded the newspaper and laid it on the table beside his place setting.

Father leveled a look on him.

"I had my annual physical a few weeks ago," Valentin said. "I'm as healthy as a horse." He wasn't the one who spent his life drinking and carousing and doing who-knew-what. Let Mother worry about his brother. Not Valentin.

"She's worried about your emotional health." Father grimaced. "I can't believe I just said that."

Valentin could. Mother was demanding and to-the-point. She had to be as reigning queen. But Father... Father had a sun-hardened facade that hid a soul sensitive enough that he was often the emissary Mother sent when she needed someone tactful.

Which meant the eighteen month reprieve Valentin had received was over.

The bite of eggs Benedict he'd put in his mouth turned to ash. It would be impolite to spit it out, even though it felt like he would vomit if he swallowed.

He swallowed anyway. Everyone said his heart was made of stone. Maybe the lining of his stomach was, too.

"Max phoned you, too?"

Dad's head came up, his eyes sharp. "No. He called you?"

Oh. He should've just asked Dad what was going

on with Mother, not revealed something he'd rather have kept quiet.

"A few times. He left voicemails." Which Valentin had deleted without listening to. As far as he was concerned, his brother no longer existed.

But the curiosity and disappointment his father couldn't quite hide cut.

Valentin couldn't help the hit of guilt before he buried it. Max deserved what he got. Valentin never wanted to see him again, and he'd said so right to his brother's face.

But despite the fact that Max was a screw-up, Mother and Father didn't feel the same way.

"He probably blew through his allowance for the month," Valentin said grimly.

Tiny lines fanned his father's eyes. He hummed noncommittally.

It was time for a subject change. If Father called Max later to find out what bind his younger brother had gotten into, Valentin didn't want to know about it.

"If it wasn't that, what exactly has Mother worried?"

Now it was Father who laid down his fork. "We can talk about it later."

Or never. Never would be Valentin's preference.

Unfortunately, his mother was used to the entire

country bowing to her wishes. And even if Father delayed, it wouldn't be long before Valentin discovered whatever this was.

"Tell me," he said.

If he wasn't mistaken, Father winced.

Valentin braced himself, imagining an invisible joist and braces shoring up the crumbling brick wall that was inside him.

"Your mother thinks it might be time to start dating again."

"What?" His voice shook slightly. His insides too, as if a light earthquake had rumbled through the foundation Valentin's being.

"It's going on two years."

Eighteen months and two days. Only that long since the day his younger brother had betrayed him. Or at least since the day Valentin had discovered the betrayal. Valentin had been completed blindsided, but it wasn't out of the realm of possibility that Max and Annika had been together behind his back for far longer.

Valentin had been devoted to Annika. Besotted with her. Blind to her faults. Or maybe that had been willful on his part.

His first duty was to his country. He'd told her that on their second date, insulated in a tiny, private booth at a coffee shop in Paris, where they'd met.

He'd been in France on business, a meeting with the prime minister.

Annika had claimed to understand, to admire his dedication to his people. But all his trips overseas, the endless parliament meetings, the late nights spent reading the newest proposed bill or trade agreement instead of being out on the town...

Annika had strayed, right into his brother's arms.

And stayed there, apparently, even though Max's longest relationship before her had had a shelf life of two weeks.

Thinking about dating again, about allowing someone into his life, made Valentin think he might yet see the return of his eggs Benedict.

Stone stomach. He attempted a smile at his father, even as his mind raced for the right answer. He folded the linen napkin in his lap, took his time placing the perfect square that emerged under his fingers onto the table beside his plate.

"I am much too busy with matters of importance to this country." That sounded too stiff, formal. Father was going to see right through him. "Dating would be too much of a distraction."

Father's pointed gaze missed nothing. "You've always felt the responsibility of the crown. But lately you've been burying yourself in your duties. Even before—you know."

Valentin's smile grew thin. "Is that Mother's opinion or yours?"

Father didn't show any sign he felt the blow, though Valentin had meant the words as a strike. His father's gaze was intent, and maybe a little sad.

"How long has it been since you took some time for yourself? Thought about something other than tariffs and treaties?"

Every night. Every night when he wondered what he might've done differently to make Annika happy. Where he'd gone wrong in his relationship with Max. How could his brother have betrayed him like he had?

But that wasn't what Father meant.

"The crown does not sleep." It was one of Mother's favorite sayings. When he'd been a young boy and asked why Mother and Father got to stay up late when he had to be tucked in early, she'd used it frequently. Later, when he'd asked why they didn't vacation abroad like some of his friends did, his Mother had answered, "The crown doesn't vacation."

"Your mother sleeps," Father said. "She relies on her staff when she needs to and she understands that if she works twenty-four hours a day, she's going to burn out. She was close to it when we met, you know. Burying all of herself in her duties because her father was dying and she didn't know how to handle it."

What was left of Valentin's smile was scraps. No doubt his bared teeth would've terrified a lesser mortal than his father. "Then it is a good thing you're in excellent health."

Father opened his mouth, no doubt to explain that hadn't been what he'd meant.

Valentin pushed back from the table, though he didn't stand. "I am not burning out. I have always loved my country, our people. I do my best to serve them diligently. Mother should recognize that." He nearly choked on his next words. "I'm only twenty-five. There is plenty of time for dating. Later. There's no royal decree that says I have to be married by thirty."

He knew, because he'd once looked. He'd been ten and Max nine when his younger brother had convinced him there was a marriage agreement that had required he marry the daughter of a visiting German dignitary, a horrid little girl who treated the servants nastily and stuck out her tongue at him whenever no adults were looking.

"You're going to have to let someone in eventually," Father said.

Valentin pictured his wall again, and his heart, which he imagined as a crumbling castle behind it. It had been bombed to the foundations. Valentin had built walls to protect it, but there was nothing there to protect anymore. He had no heart to give.

"Does she have someone in mind?" Until Annika, he'd expected to make a political match. Marry to unite two counties and all of that. He couldn't imagine trusting anyone else with the deepest parts of himself, but if it was for his country, maybe he could bear it.

But Father shook his head and wore an expression of faint... chagrin?

"What?" Valentin's tone became sharper as his temper got shorter. He stood, straightening his shirt cuffs. He had a meeting in an hour and needed to prepare.

"She's got this idea that..." Father shook his head. He stood too, his height a reminder of how much Valentin admired the man.

"Tell me," Valentin repeated, temper dissipating like sand in a windstorm. Father didn't deserve that from him. It wasn't Father who'd betrayed him. It wasn't Father's fault his heart didn't exist.

"She heard about this high profile matchmaker lady."

"Absolutely not." The words were out before Valentin had time to think them through. It was a ludicrous idea. Out of the question.

Was that what Mother thought of his skill at attracting the opposite sex? That he needed someone to pick a match for him?

"I'll tell her myself," Valentin said grimly. "There will be no matchmaker for me."

Crystal Ramos drove her compact car away from the gatehouse and parked where she'd been directed, beside the royal garage. Was there a different name for it if the garage was so massive it could've fit her apartment inside at least ten times?

She'd been invited to the castle to visit Glorvaird's royal family. Well, part of it.

She was still mired in disbelief as she got out of the car. She stood on the pavers, craning her neck up to admire the castle that rose above her on two sides.

She couldn't believe she was here. Or that Queen Eloise had even heard of her.

Her! A nobody from a family of nobodies. She hadn't even finished college. And the queen had called her *directly*. Not some assistant. Not an email.

She was here to meet with the crown prince because he *needed her services*.

If she could find the prince a perfect match, she'd have her choice of future clients. She'd never have to work with sniveling, spoiled men like Ronald Frothingham again.

And maybe—this dream was so far out there that she hadn't really let it coalesce as a thought until this very moment—maybe she wouldn't have to worry about every single penny. She could pay Michael and Reid's college tuition and be able to eat more than ramen with a side of ramen. She could buy lobster.

She was shaken out of her daydream at a polite cough from nearby.

"Oh, hi!" She pushed away from the car, where she'd leaned as her happy daydreams had spun around her.

A man—not the prince—in a dove gray sweater over a starched collared shirt and pressed slacks was waiting near the corner of the garage, where a footpath led around the side.

"Sorry, I was woolgathering." Could he really blame her? She'd jumped at the chance to meet with the prince, but the only time available in his calendar had been early in the day. She'd always considered anything before seven a.m. ridiculous, but she couldn't exactly say that to her newest client, not with everything that was riding on this.

The well-dressed man was still waiting on her as

she dragged her leather laptop bag out of the back-seat of her car.

When she joined him, he said, "This way, miss."

She'd hoped there was a second door, maybe a servant's entrance or something, around the corner—she'd seen the main entrance at the front of the garage—but that hope was dashed as she followed the guy down the footpath around the base of the stone castle.

She'd worn a knee-length skirt and a button-up blouse with her best pair of black heels. They weren't Louboutins, or even knockoffs, but she was hoping the ensemble made her look professional and conservative. As it was, the humidity was creeping in beneath her skirt and making her underarms damp. Or maybe that was her nerves.

She tried to unobtrusively wipe her palms on her skirt.

And then the stone footpath gave way to sand as the castle wall ended and the ocean opened up in front of them, a panorama that spanned the horizon.

Her escort kept going.

"Uh, excuse me."

She stalled out on the last stone paver.

Her guide turned back and raised one imperious eyebrow.

She wondered what she'd gotten into. This was

someone who worked for the prince. Did her client have that same superior attitude? Or worse?

Was he going to be another Ronald?

She made herself focus. "Let's start over, shall we? I'm Crystal."

She extended her hand and, after a prolonged moment, he shook it. "Conrad, the crown prince's personal assistant."

Ah. Gatekeeper, schedule keeper. The prince's man.

Not someone she wanted to offend.

"Conrad. It's nice to meet you. Where are we going?"

"Your meeting with his highness."

"On the beach?"

Her skepticism must've been audible because Conrad sighed with a good dose of long-suffering. She'd heard sighs like that often from her younger brothers.

"If you would...?" He gestured for her to follow him.

And even though a small part of her wondered if this was some elaborate joke Michael had cooked up —did her brother have the connections to pull this off?—she reached down and took off her shoes and followed Conrad onto the sand.

The sun was coming up over the edge of the

water. The sky was all orange hues. Even the sand was gilded gold.

She blamed the romantic lighting for what happened next.

It felt like a lightning bolt. A current that zapped straight down her spine to her toes when she caught sight of the prince.

He was shirtless, his skin slicked with sweat and gleaming bronze as he jogged down the beach at the water's edge.

No, jogging wasn't the right term. There was someone a few paces behind the prince—a bodyguard?—who was puffing for air and straining for each step as he fought to keep up.

Sprinting. That was the word.

The crown prince was sprinting closer and closer, each step churning up sand behind him.

She'd known he was handsome. Yesterday, she'd pored over her computer for hours, surfing the internet and reading article after article about him. Of course there had been pictures. She was acquainted with the planes of his face, the patrician nose, the startling ice-blue of his eyes.

But this was not the polished, handsome man in a designer suit, posing for photos. Even in the occasional candid she'd seen, he was all elegant haughtiness.

This was the prince like she'd never seen him before. And she guessed not many people had.

And then he raised a hand and did a slow lope right toward them.

Lightning bolt. Prince with a hot bod. Crystal blinked as she felt a blush scalding her cheeks. She had one-point-five seconds to find her composure, but it had deserted her completely.

Think about Michael and Reid. Her brothers needed her. She needed this job.

She breathed in deeply the scent of salt water, and when she exhaled, she was back to herself.

A few yards away, the prince slowed to a walk. It didn't seem fair that he was only slightly winded. He glanced at her, his eyes wary, as he approached Conrad first.

His assistant held out a T-shirt, which the prince slipped over his head, the material quickly covering his powerful chest and the six-pack she hadn't imagined beneath his tailored suits.

Conrad handed him a small towel that he used to wipe first his face and then his hands.

And then the prince turned from Conrad to her.

"So you're the matchmaker."

"So I am." She stepped forward to meet his handshake and only belatedly remembered she had her shoes in hand. She juggled them, along with her satchel, her face heating again at her own awkwardness, before she got everything into her left hand.

She couldn't help the lift of her chin. Meeting on the beach had been his idea, not hers. "I'm Crystal Ramos. It's an honor to meet you, your highness."

He handed the towel to Conrad, who faded back, presumably heading off the beach. Which left only the two of them and the bodyguard, who stood several feet away, scanning the view back toward the castle.

The prince's grip was warm and sure. "Valentin, if you please."

If she pleased. To be on a first name basis with the prince.

But as he squeezed her hand once and then released her, she saw that the wariness in his expression hadn't disappeared. It'd been joined by curiosity, maybe. But it was still there.

It had been his mother who'd called her, not the prince himself. Of course he was wary.

He nodded back the direction she and Conrad had come from, and she fell into step beside him.

"Your highness. I mean... Valentin." That was going to take some getting used to.

His strides were so long that she had to scramble in the sand to keep up with him. She grasped for professionalism.

"Thank you for meeting with me," she said.

"I'm afraid I don't have long." And his gaze was distant. As if he'd already dismissed her. "Frankly, hiring you was my mother's idea."

She knew that, but she hadn't expected his curt dismissal.

All the dreams she'd been spinning began to shimmer like a mirage. She felt a tremble start deep inside but masked it with a polite smile.

"And you're going along with it?" *Am I wasting my time?*

They'd reached the edge of the castle wall, where the sand met the stone pavers.

He turned to her.

And she realized she was standing with her only empty hand cocked on her hip. Probably it wasn't appropriate to speak to the prince with an attitude, but she didn't like feeling misled. The queen had insinuated that the job was Crystal's.

"I'll give you four dates. With different women or the same one, I don't care. Wow me."

What arrogance!

She opened her mouth to tell him exactly where he could put his *wow me*, but what emerged was, "What are you looking for in a match?"

Chapter Two

Crystal hadn't been kicked out. She guessed that was something.

Her feet were hurting, and she was regretting the heels for the second time as she followed the prince and his assistant up at least two flights of stone stairs and down a series of twisting passageways.

The prince—she still couldn't think of him as Valentin—had asked her to bear with him as he spoke to Conrad. Which left her to follow and watch the rapid-fire interplay as Conrad flicked through an iPad while he spoke of engagements that the prince either accepted or rejected. There was a reminder about a new bill parliament was reviewing before Conrad handed him a single sheet of paper as they reached a doorway cut from the stone. Then the prince opened the door and held it for her as Conrad peeled off down the hallway.

"Uh, thanks." She slipped by him, getting a blast of his body heat as she passed. Inside was a sitting room that was so formal it reminded her of her grandma's parlor. There were no knickknacks or doilies here, but the air was still *don't touch*. She gave the dark, square sofa the side-eye but followed the prince through an adjoining doorway.

This room was an office. Light streamed in from a window cut into the wide stone castle exterior, illuminating floor-to-ceiling bookcases along two interior walls. They were stuffed with what looked like boring legal tomes. No novels in sight, sadly.

The prince used a remote to turn on a large flat-screen telly, and a national news channel came to life. The volume was so low it was hardly audible. He barely glanced at it before moving behind the desk, which was massive and carved out of some kind of heavy wood. It was neat, almost bare. Only a few papers were scattered across the surface along with a closed laptop. The paper Conrad had given the prince joined the others.

He didn't sit in the comfy-looking leather chair behind the desk but stood with one hand planted on the wooden surface.

"When can we schedule the first date?"

Oh yes. He was going to be as high maintenance as Ronald. At least he was handsome. And a catch, all things considered.

Think about the rewards. She could do this. For Michael and Reid.

"Do you mind if I sit?" she asked.

She didn't wait for him to answer but perched on the chair on this side of the desk. She opened her bag and vacillated between the laptop and the notepad. Notepad it was. She flipped to a clean sheet of paper.

"What are you looking for in a woman?"

His expression instantly closed off. "That's what you want to ask me? We're not doing a questionnaire from a dating site. I agreed to four dates. You provide the match."

She smiled tightly. "How am I supposed to find you a match if I don't know what kind of person you're looking for? Do you want to meet someone you can talk to about current events? Politics? What level of affection are you most comfortable with? If you like her, how often do you want to see her?"

The prince was still leaning on his desk, but his smile had turned brittle. "Miss Ramos."

"Crystal."

"Crystal. I'm sure you're aware of my history."

Of course she was. The breakup with his fiancée had been public and ugly. Although all of the media coverage had been gathered from Valentin's brother and his ex-fiancée. Valentin himself had never answered an interview question about what happened. Never spoken badly about them or how he must've been hurt by the whole thing.

Several articles had accused him of having a heart of stone. Being uncaring, because the prince had gone on as if everything was business as usual. Who knew if it was true?

She met his stare squarely. "I don't read gossip rags, but it's impossible not to know that something happened."

Now his expression turned grim. "So it is. I imagine every eligible single woman in the country knows."

She considered him. "So you've given up on finding someone."

If so, he presented a challenge that she'd never faced before. All of her previous clients had at least *believed* in love. They'd even wanted to find it. If Valentin didn't, would she be wasting her time?

So you've given up on finding someone.

Though he was supposed to be made of stone,

Valentin felt like his insides were a pot, merrily simmering away on the stovetop. Every push from the pretty young matchmaker felt as if she was turning up the heat on the burner.

He'd been the one to bring up Annika and Max, and now it felt as if his lid was rattling. Ready to blow off if he didn't release some steam. His regular morning run was supposed to have done that, but it hadn't helped.

What could he say to make her understand?

I trusted them both, and look what happened.

That wouldn't be helpful. She'd probably tell him to see a therapist.

Annika was my true love.

In hindsight, he could admit that there were things about her that had driven him crazy. Surely he'd done the same to her. If she'd only talked to him, maybe they could've worked things out.

I have nothing left to give.

The truest answer of all, but one he wasn't about to share with this virtual stranger—or anybody for that matter.

He never should have brought the matchmaker up here. He'd agreed to the meeting because Mother had pushed. He'd meant to dismiss her quickly, but she'd surprised him with her sass, and something underneath her attitude made him think of kicking a puppy when he'd wanted to turn her off.

He'd said the words agreeing to four dates without thinking. He was a man of his word. He'd go through with them. But he wasn't going to find a match.

"I'm quite over what happened with my brother." His cool tone gave voice to the lie, but he couldn't look at her as he said it. He flipped open his laptop, unlocking it with a few keystrokes. It was a matter of a few seconds to pull up his diary.

"I have a state dinner a week from today. I'll bring a guest of your choice. You can make arrangements with Conrad. She'll need to be cleared by palace security."

She stared at him as if he'd lost his marbles. Maybe he had.

"You want to take a first date to a state dinner? I assume it's black tie."

He nodded.

"And you want me to choose someone for you after a fifteen minute meeting?"

"Is that a problem?" He hadn't fired her, but maybe she would quit.

He could see the wheels turning in her mind. There was a tiny part of him that wondered if she could do it, could find someone to bring his heart to life again.

Then he dismissed the thought. He would settle for companionship. That was enough. It had to be.

"If you don't mind, I have a full schedule today." He knew he was being rude, but he didn't apologize.

"Fine." There was fire in her eyes as she stood and straightened her skirt. In the blouse and business attire, he wouldn't have given her a second glance if he'd seen her at an event or in public.

But there was a spray of freckles across the bridge of her nose that he'd noticed on the beach, and now he'd couldn't stop noticing them.

She was utterly unremarkable, except for those freckles.

He decided he didn't like them.

"Thank you for your time," she said stiffly. She flounced from the room. A moment later, he realized she'd left her bag on the floor beside her chair.

He heard the outer door open and close.

No matter. He'd have Conrad return the bag to her.

His desk phone rang with the distinct tone that meant it was his private line, one that only a handful of people had access to.

He picked it up without glancing at the display.

"Valentin. Don't hang up."

Max.

Hearing his brother's voice brought back a visceral memory of those last moments. Annika's lips, swollen and bee-stung after kissing his brother. Max's flashing, unapologetic stare. The crippling pain of betrayal.

"What part of 'I never want to speak to you again' was unclear to you?"

Was that his voice? He sounded as cold as ice. He felt anything but. His collar was too tight. He tugged, but then remembered it was a T-shirt. His run and the momentary calm he'd felt as his feet pounded the sand was long gone.

"I screwed up."

At least Max was admitting it. It was small comfort.

"I need to see you. There's something—"

Valentin let loose an expletive. "No."

"Val, I know we hurt you—"

"Don't call me again."

He hung up the phone with ruthless force. And when it rang instantly, he knew it was Max again.

He took it off the cradle and mashed the switch-hook, then released it. If Max called back, he'd get a busy signal. He was already blocked from Valentin's cell phone.

He tossed the receiver onto the desk, ignoring the clatter it made.

He was threading both hands into his hair, elbows above his head, when he realized Crystal was hovering in the doorway.

He let his arms drop to his sides.

She was watching him with unconcealed curiosity. And pity.

He didn't want her pity.

"You'll forget you just witnessed that." He made it an order, channeling his mother more than he'd ever done before.

She ignored him, bending to retrieve her bag from the floor.

"I'm sorry," she said faintly, and slipped out the door.

For what? Sorry she'd taken him on as a client? Sorry she'd witnessed a private moment, witnessed his temper exploding? Or sorry for him?

Because he was a lousy excuse for a human being.

Hours after the disastrous meeting with the matchmaker, Valentin was striding down the castle corridor when he nearly ran over his cousin Tirith.

"Sorry," he muttered.

"Me too." Her smile was genuine but muted.

"All right?" he asked. He and Tirith had grown somewhat close in the past few years. Over a year ago, she'd accidentally gotten in an auto accident that had resulted in a little girl's life-altering injuries. Before that, Tirith had been lively and free-spirited. Since then, she'd grown reserved and quiet. He quite missed her fervor for life.

"I'm fine," she said, but the shadows behind her eyes remained. "Are you all right?"

And there was a part of him that wanted to see her old smile. "Mother has hired a matchmaker for me."

"What?" She burst out the word in a single giggle before she remembered herself.

He shrugged. "She thinks it's time I started dating again."

Tirith's gaze was maybe too sharp. "What do you think?"

"I suppose I can't be alone forever." But he wasn't exactly in a hurry to meet someone. "What about you? You haven't dated since Moreno."

"I never really dated Luc."

That wasn't what it had looked like. She'd been close with the man, attending functions and inspiring media speculation as to their relationship status. But when Tirith had desperately needed to hide out for a few days, she'd asked her twin sister to switch places with her. And Moreno had promptly fallen for the Texas twin.

"I'd be more than happy to divert the matchmaker's attention to you."

Tirith laughed, as he'd hoped she would. "Not necessary. And good luck."

He'd need it if he was going to get through this unscathed.

Chapter Three

"I had fun tonight."

A week after his first meeting with the matchmaker, Valentin stood looking down at his date, Amy. The state dinner had been surprisingly painless. It was over now, and he'd escorted her out to the drive, where the day limo would return her home. There were still a few state officials lingering on the lawn, their cars waiting on the drive while they conversed. It was a public place for a goodbye.

He was thankful for that. It meant he didn't have to decipher her social clues. Figure out whether a kiss was appropriate or a hug would be better. Here, it was appropriate for him to tuck her into the limo and say a simple good-night.

There was a reason Annika had been his only long-term relationship.

His social skills left much to be desired. He could work a room of politicians, but reading a woman was something he'd never mastered.

"Thank you for coming," he said.

Amy smiled at him, her eyes kind and intelligent.

"I won't wait for you to call," she said with a pat to his cheek.

She got in the limo without a backward glance, and he closed the door for her, watching as she drove off.

Her intelligence had drawn him to her when they'd met in a university chemistry lab more than five years ago now. He and Amy had gone on all of two dates when they'd realized they were better off as friends.

But he had to hand it to Crystal. She'd done her homework. It was true that the media documented every time he was seen in public, but it must've taken hours of reading internet articles to find the mention of those dates from his sophomore year. Or maybe she'd just phoned his mother to ask.

It had been nice to catch up with Amy. She didn't have a royal lineage, but she was interesting and educated. She'd held her own talking tax law with the attorney sitting to her right while Valentin had been engaged with the woman's husband, a high ranking official from a neighboring country.

Amy had been demure and charming and kept conversation flowing all evening long.

If there had been any spark between them, he'd already be texting her for a second date.

Instead, he was considering whether he should text Crystal.

He hadn't been able to stop thinking about her since she'd walked out of his suite a week ago. He blamed Max for the stain on what would've been an otherwise uneventful, if uncomfortable, meeting.

But his anger at Max didn't explain why he was still thinking about *her* even now as he nodded a last good-bye to guests and strode past the pair of body-guards standing at the entrance to the hallway that led to the royal family's private residence.

He was only paying half attention to his surroundings as he pulled his phone from his pocket and fired off a text.

Nice try. No chemistry. Who's next?

His phone beeped as he entered his rooms, pulling loose his bow tie.

I saw.

He had to bite back a smile. Events like the state dinner were televised on a remote channel that had to be special ordered from a viewer's cable provider. The local news would likely have a short clip of him shaking the ambassador's hand and little more. But if Crystal had been watching, it meant she'd worked for it.

He let the door close behind him, sealing him in privacy.

And dialed the phone.

Crystal answered with a blush.

Which was incredibly silly, given that the prince couldn't see through the device to catch her in her pajama pants and oversize T-shirt, nor could he see the evidence of the now-empty bowl of chocolate ice cream or popcorn kernels that littered the coffee table in her tiny flat.

She hadn't thought watching the state dinner on telly would have been as interesting as one of her favorite rom-coms, but she'd been riveted.

"At least you were polite," she said by way of greeting.

The prince had been the epitome of a perfect date, escorting Amy around the room, introducing her, making conversation. Crystal had been a little surprised by his good manners after he'd admitted that hiring her was his mother's idea.

But like he'd said in his text, anyone with eyes could see there was no heat between them. No spark.

"You mean like I wasn't to you last week?"

It took her a second to remember what he'd said, to figure out what he meant. Polite. He wasn't talking about their chemistry.

As he shouldn't be. It had all been one-sided. Her side. And who wouldn't be attracted to the prince after seeing him in all his post-exercise glory?

"I didn't take it personally," she said. It hadn't been her best client meeting, but it hadn't had to be.

She'd spoken on the phone to her brother Michael earlier in the week and sworn him to secrecy before she'd revealed her job. And he'd pointed out that even if she didn't make a match for the prince, she'd have him as a client for her CV.

She'd prefer to make Valentin a success story, but she'd take what she could get. Especially since he didn't want to cooperate.

"I still feel I owe you an apology."

That was unexpected.

"I'll take it. I don't suppose you'll give me a hint as to what kind of woman you'd like to meet next?"

"I rather think I'd like to be surprised."

He might like that, but it made things more difficult for her. She mentally went through her list of single friends. Maybe Angelica would like to be set up with the prince. If he wasn't taking this seriously, she *could* do it...

"I'm supposed to visit an elementary school on Friday. Promote literacy and all that. Do you think you could send someone to come along with me?"

Three days? That was short notice.

But it wasn't as if she could refuse. "I'll do my best. Will you be doing a reading? Or just a speech?"

He cleared his throat. "Does that matter?"

She laughed a little, awkwardly. "Only to assuage my own curiosity."

She wasn't obsessed with the royals like some people she saw posting on social media, but she'd known about the prince's work to promote childhood literacy since he'd walked into the public eye as a teenager.

There was an audible pause and then, "If you'd like to come along, you'd be welcome. In the background, with Conrad."

"Of course."

Because she worked for him. Or for the queen, although the lines were awfully blurry. Employees stayed in the background, while whomever she set him up with would be front and center.

She swallowed back the irrational disappointment. "I'll check my schedule."

"Fine."

"I should go."

He said good-night and she tossed her phone. It bounced off the couch cushions and onto the floor, hitting the wood with a clatter. She didn't bother to pick it up but paced the small living room and into the kitchen, then whirled around to fetch her dirty dishes.

Valentin was being kind, not putting her in her place, even if that's what it had felt like.

He'd called her, after all, and she was attracted to him.

It didn't take a rocket scientist to figure out what was going on here.

Even as a small child, Crystal had spun daydreams. Grand ones.

Being an astronaut and going to the moon.

Dancing in a Russian ballet company.

Having a prince fall in love with her.

She needed to be very careful here. Valentin had zero interest in her. She was in his sphere for one reason only.

To find him a match.

Besides, she wasn't looking for love for herself. Her last breakup had been messy—shouting match and ugly crying messy. She'd believed Harry had been *the one,* and she'd been devastated to find out he hadn't felt the same about her.

She'd go back on the market eventually, but not yet.

Not only would she be humiliated if Valentin figured out she had a crush on him, if there was any hint of scandal, the royal family would put the kibosh on her using them on her CV.

The royal stamp of approval would give her fledgling business validation when she desperately needed it.

She couldn't mess this up.

Whatever attraction she harbored for Valentin needed to be crushed. Pronto.

Valentin hung up the phone, while using his other hand to rub his chest.

Something felt off.

Not wrong. Just different.

He couldn't place it.

He began his nightly routine. Checked his messages and emails. Nothing from his mother or Conrad that was urgent enough it couldn't wait until tomorrow. He plugged his phone into its charger in his office and retired to his rooms, where he turned on a sitcom that allowed him some time to be mindless.

But he couldn't get rid of the sensation that something had changed.

And it hadn't happened on the date, as pleasant as seeing Amy had been.

It was the phone call with Crystal that bothered him. When she'd asked if he would be reading to the kids.

She'd sounded as if... as if she admired him.

And why shouldn't she? He was doing a good thing. A lot of people admired him.

But it was different because it was Crystal.

From the very beginning, she hadn't cut him any slack. He could still picture her standing in the sand, clutching her shoes with her hand propped on her hip.

He glanced in the mirror just before he raised his toothbrush to his mouth.

He was smiling.

Because of Crystal.

He put his toothbrush back down, stared at himself in the mirror.

What had just happened?

He was thinking about a woman and smiling. Looking forward to seeing her again.

Crystal had done what he'd thought was impossible.

She'd awakened his heart. Sure, it was still barricaded behind an impenetrable wall.

But he'd thought it was DOA. Buried with a headstone.

Crystal was only doing a job for him. He wasn't interested in her. Not really.

But if he could smile about her antics, maybe he could fall in love again. Someday. With someone. Far into the future.

Chapter Four

Valentin wasn't feeling well.

Crystal could tell from his pallor and the flush in his cheeks.

But he was playacting that nothing was wrong as he read to the children, a mix of kindergarteners and first graders. He should look silly wedged into the chair meant for a small child, but he'd stretched his long legs out in front of him and crossed his ankles. The children were hanging on every word.

So was she.

So was his date.

She *had* recruited a friend to be Valentin's match for the day. Pansy was more of an acquaintance, someone Crystal had met when matching a millionaire CEO over a year ago. She'd done an initial round of interviews for each dating candidate, and she and Pansy had hit it off. Their friendship had grown to the occasional coffee date. She was an entrepreneur and one of the smartest women Crystal knew.

She'd spent the first few minutes of the classroom visit chatting with the children while Valentin spoke to the teacher. She'd been a big hit, judging by the giggles and awestruck gazes she was still getting.

While Crystal was standing at the back of the classroom, sandwiched between Conrad and a beefy bodyguard. She almost hadn't come. But then she'd wondered what Valentin would think if she didn't show up.

And the school was only a few minutes' walk from her apartment.

She was worried about Valentin. "He needs to cancel his other engagements for the day," she muttered under her breath.

"He won't," Conrad returned.

Valentin concluded his reading with a charming smile, and the children buzzed around him, their small voices clamoring for attention.

"Can you read us another one?" one little girl asked.

"My mom says she's in love wiff you!"

"I got a scrape on my knee. Wanna see it?"

Valentin smiled through it all, though his smile had grown tighter over the half hour they'd been in this classroom.

The teacher clapped her hands, and the kids quieted.

She thanked Valentin, and he and Pansy excused themselves.

The bodyguard was the first person into the hall, and Crystal hung back with Conrad as the prince and his date walked down the hallway empty of children.

Valentin and Pansy had their heads tipped close together, and Crystal forced herself to avert her eyes. Look at that artwork by creative little ones. The black and red blobs drawn in crayon were... well, she didn't know what they were supposed to be exactly, but they were something.

The bright noonday sunlight made her eyes tear as they exited the school building. Another bodyguard stood outside on the sidewalk, and Valentin's red convertible was parked at the curb. Two motorcycles for the bodyguards were parked right behind it. Valentin was supposed to drive Pansy to a coffeeshop to chat.

But as a small crowd of onlookers watched from across the street, Valentin leaned in and kissed Pansy on the cheek, and she peeled off down the sidewalk, walking briskly away with a glance over her shoulder. A lens flashed from across the street. A photographer.

Conrad hurried forward, and Crystal found herself on his heels, even though the prince wasn't her responsibility. The date was. Had he disliked Pansy so much?

But when Valentin turned to speak to Conrad, Crystal caught sight of the darker flush blazing in his cheeks and the fevered look in his eyes.

"I need a rain check," the prince said.

Before Conrad could answer, someone hailed him from the crowd across the street.

Valentin stiffened beside her. The dark-haired bodyguard moved to intercept the man—was it a man?—who was jogging toward them.

"Conrad," Valentin's voice was pained.

She realized the man approaching had something strapped to his chest. Was it a bomb? Her adrenaline surged.

The bodyguard was there, intercepting him, but if that was a bomb, weren't they in the danger zone?

"There are at least two reporters present," Conrad said. Almost like a warning.

She couldn't tear her eyes away from the bundle at the man's chest.

And then she realized it was wrapped in a fuzzy pink blanket. A baby blanket.

"It's a baby." Tears of relief pricked her eyes. "He's got a baby. Not a bomb."

She glanced at the men to find Conrad looking at her as if she'd spoken Swahili. Valentin hadn't looked away from the approaching man.

"It's okay," he called out to the bodyguard, who glanced back at him and then let the guy through.

And she realized why the man looked familiar.

It was Max. Valentin's brother.

Oh no.

She glanced at Conrad, and this time they were on the same page. They needed to get Valentin out of there.

More people had gathered, some on this side of the street. They were watching and pointing and whispering.

Valentin seemed frozen in place as Max approached. He stared at the bundle at his brother's chest.

Max had several days' scruff at his chin and looked more rumpled than she'd ever seen him in photographs.

He glanced briefly at her and Conrad but didn't waver from his course toward his brother.

"What are you doing here?" Valentin asked.

She'd heard that same cold tone in his voice in his office that first morning.

"I told you, I need to talk to you."

The baby let out a wail, and Valentin jerked.

"Meet your niece. Clara."

Valentin stood still and expressionless. A muscle jumped in his cheek.

Max exhaled loudly, looking off to the side. "This isn't easy, is it?" he said. "I'm sorry."

He sounded genuine. But Crystal didn't know the man. Maybe he was a consummate liar.

Valentin didn't respond.

A shout from behind them drew Crystal's attention. The crowd was pressing closer. Perhaps they'd sniffed out a family scandal unfolding right before their eyes. The bodyguard was using himself as a buffer, arms outstretched to keep the people at bay. But one man wasn't going to stand long against that many people.

"Get him out of here." Conrad pressed something cold into her hand. Car keys. Then he joined the bodyguard to try and hold back the press of people.

She moved behind Valentin and touched his arm. He surprised her by gripping her hand. He was burning up, his skin hot to the touch.

"We need to leave," she murmured.

Max's gaze fixed on their joined hands. "Who's this?" His smile was genuine, not flirtatious.

But Valentin bared his teeth, his entire body going tense. He started to pull away as if he were preparing to throw a punch.

"Don't—" she said quietly.

And maybe it was her softly spoken word that broke him out of his distracted state. Or maybe he finally heard the crowd calling out behind them.

She tugged his hand, and he let her pull him toward the car.

"Stay away from me," he spat at his brother.

She hadn't intended to get in the car, but the flush on his face and the way his hand shook on the doorframe altered her decision. "Get in," he demanded.

She didn't want to argue, so she slid onto the smooth leather seats.

He rounded the car and climbed in, then took the keys from her when she offered them.

He could put her out of the car around the corner, when they put some distance between themselves and this craziness.

Valentin seemed to have the same idea, because he turned the corner and pulled over two blocks down.

He slid the car into a parallel spot smoothly, shoved the gearshift into park.

She was going to excuse herself, promise not to mention his brother, but he gripped the top of the steering wheel with both hands and bowed forward to press his forehead against his wrists.

"How—?" he gasped the word. She couldn't make out if he was crying or just upset.

She couldn't leave him there like that, not without Conrad or a bodyguard or someone.

She reached out to comfort him, touching his shoulder. She could feel that he was burning up even through his shirt.

"Your fever is out of control," she said. "My apartment is nearby. Why don't you come up? At least take some ibuprofen or something to bring the fever down."

He only grunted in response.

Valentin couldn't remember feeling this miserable, ever. He'd had his share of head colds and even the flu once or twice, but none of them compared to this. Right now, his head felt like it was going to explode, and chills racked his entire body.

That was the only reason he allowed Crystal to

drag him bodily across the street, through a vine-covered alleyway, and up a back staircase.

Or maybe it wasn't so much her dragging him as him leaning on her so he could remain upright.

He'd felt it coming on this morning but thought he could power through it. He'd gotten steadily worse while they were at the school and told his date —Petunia?—that he'd love to see her again another time. And then the full force of this illness had struck when he'd come face to face with Max. He'd felt like he'd been hit by a bus.

"I didn't punch him, did I?" he asked. "I was just thinking about it..."

Crystal stumbled on the top step, almost toppling them both into a door that was painted bright red.

"You didn't punch him," she confirmed with a grunt as she tried to maneuver her key into the door.

"Not this time," he muttered.

Her keys rattled against the knob, and then they were inside. It was much cooler here. Her A/C was doing a good job battling the late-spring heat.

She gave him a full-body nudge toward a sofa beneath a long window. Yes. He wanted to be lying there. And then he was, although he was a little fuzzy on how he'd gotten horizontal.

"You hit him before?" she asked. Her voice was far off and muffled by the sound of running water.

Were his eyes closed? They were. The darkness was nice. Then he couldn't see her judgment.

"I hit him. It didn't make me feel better. Just hurt my hand."

"Yeah. That's kinda how it works." She was whispering now. Something damp and cool touched his forehead. "Can you sit up? Just a little. Here."

She put a hand beneath his arm as he pushed up on a wobbly elbow. She gave him some pills and a cool drink of water and then let him lie back down.

He imagined that she brushed the hair back from his forehead.

But it was a nice thing to imagine, so he told her, "It's not supposed to hurt me."

"What hurts?" Her voice was closer than he thought it should be. Was she sitting on the floor next to him? She seemed close. He tried to open his eyes and check but they wouldn't cooperate. "Your hand?"

"No. M'heart." He was slurring a little. If he could sleep off this awful headache, he'd wake up and find it was all a dream. No Max. No baby. No pain thudding through him with each beat of his heart. "I've got a heart of stone, haven't you heard? That's what everyone says."

But if that was true, why did it hurt so badly?

"Shh. You should rest." She touched him again. A brush of her fingers against his temple. And then her voice was far away. "Conrad? He's in my apartment. Not very coherent. No, he's fine, I think. Burning up. They did what? No, no he can stay here. No one would think to look for him here. You can send a guard." She rattled off an address and then she was quiet.

He liked her. Probably too much. He didn't want to like her. Or anyone else. If he let someone else in, he might get hurt again.

But then he wouldn't have anyone to nurse him, either. No one to ply him with pain relievers and cool water. To brush his hair off his forehead.

He was arguing with himself over the finer points when the darkness finally took him.

He woke in the night, throwing off the blanket that weighted him down and pulling at his shirt that felt like it was suffocating him.

And Crystal was there again, with medicine and cool water, unbuttoning his shirt when his fingers wouldn't work. He hated to leave his undershirt on when it stuck to his body with sickly sweat, but his sense of propriety wouldn't let him strip down in her apartment. He asked her to flip on the news, but she refused.

He got all imperial on her, demanding it. But since he was as weak as a baby, there was nothing he could do when she refused to fetch the remote and turn on the telly.

She did fetch another cool, damp washcloth. This time she laid it across his face as he leaned his head back against the couch cushions.

He fell asleep like that.

Chapter Five

When he awoke the next morning, Valentin was disoriented.

It took him several seconds to remember leaning on Crystal and coming up to her apartment in a feverish haze.

Bright sunlight was streaming through the window into his face. It was making his head pound. Or maybe that was the residual effect of the illness. He could feel the weakness of his limbs, but the fever itself seemed to be gone. Thank God.

He sat up on the couch, letting his feet hit the floor. But weakness threatened to overcome him, and he put his head in both hands, elbows on his knees.

With his head down like this, he could smell just

how badly he stank of sick and stale sweat. How embarrassing.

But Crystal didn't seem to be here. He glanced around the neat, eclectic space. Two overstuffed chairs brimming with colorful pillows. A half-sized bookshelf stuffed with novels, a small telly sitting on top of it. Separating the living area from the kitchen was a bar with stools. The walls were painted a soft blue. Pictures of her with two men, younger than she, hung on the walls. In one they were rock climbing, in another they were at the beach. In another they had their arms around each other, and they were laughing.

He suddenly realized he knew nothing about Crystal's personal life. Mother would've vetted her before she'd been hired, but Valentin had been so self-absorbed that he didn't even know if she had a family. Or a boyfriend.

Where was she?

She'd been nearby when he'd woken several times during the night, always replacing his cool washrags.

He winced when he remembered ordering her to turn on the television. Demanding it like a toddler. What a prize she must think he was.

By taking him home like she had, she'd gone

above and beyond her duty as an employee. She'd almost acted like a... friend.

And he'd treated her shabbily.

If he were lucky, she'd be sleeping right now. If he were doubly lucky, she'd forget about his actions in the night.

And then he remembered her call to Conrad. At least, he *thought* she'd called his assistant. He could've been dreaming it. She'd asked a question that niggled the back of his brain—

Max.

Remembering his brother was like receiving a punch to the solar plexus. For a few seconds, he couldn't breathe. He felt as if he'd blacked out and was seeing stars both at the same time.

Max with a baby.

There had been photographers outside the school when he'd visited. If they'd gotten a picture of Max and Valentin, the press would be in a frenzy.

And Conrad had probably told Crystal not to let him see it.

Some sick part of his brain insisted he raise his head and look around. And there was the remote, only a scant few inches away on a low, scratched coffee table.

Where was his phone? His keys? He had

options. Probably Mother and Father were trying to reach him. He could call them.

Or he could get in his car and drive as fast and as far as he could. Abdicate, even, though that would leave Max to run the country when Mother no longer could.

He'd ignored his fanciful thoughts and gotten as far as picking up the remote when Crystal walked into the room from a hallway he'd barely noticed.

She was wearing jeans and a tank top, and her feet were bare. Her hair was in a ponytail, and she didn't have a stitch of makeup on.

Those freckles.

She glanced at the remote, her gaze zeroing in on his face. "You sure you want to do that before you have coffee?"

She knew. Of course she knew.

"I—how bad is it?"

She shrugged. "I saw a couple of things pop up on my social media feeds, but I haven't turned on the news yet."

He bowed his head, though he was aware of her moving into the kitchenette area, running water, cabinets opening. And then a coffee maker quietly chugged and hissed.

He used one hand to rub his face. He felt weary, even though he'd slept.

"I've spent several weeks finessing the language in the exports bill..." He waved off his own words. She didn't care about the details of some bill parliament was trying to push through. No one else did, either. At least that's what it felt like. "And the media is probably going crazy because my brother showed up with a baby in tow."

Max was surely playing the sympathy card. Eating up the attention.

"Who knows if that was even his child," Valentin burst out. He let his hand fall away from his face, and the remote clattered to the coffee table.

And Crystal was standing right there, a glass of water in hand. She'd abandoned the kitchen and gotten an up-close view of his temper. Again.

"I'm sorry." He stood up, ignoring the stiffness in his muscles. "You always seem to see me at my worst." Humiliation heated his neck, warmth leaching up into his face. "If you'll tell me where my car keys are, I'll get out of your hair."

He made a point of not meeting her gaze. Had it only been a couple of days before when he'd been thinking how much he liked her? And now this.

She set the water glass on a side table, and the next thing he knew, she'd reached out and touched his forearm, her fingers cool and soft.

At the touch, his frantic thoughts stopped

whirling. A visceral memory fought through the haze of yesterday's chaos. Him taking her hand on the sidewalk. And knowing that because she was near, everything was going to be all right.

He looked down at the place where she touched him now, her paler skin against his tan.

And he wanted to hold her hand again. He needed it.

So he moved the few inches it took to clasp her hand in his.

For one blissful moment, everything else fell away. There was no Max, no royal duty, no scandal.

Only Crystal, only the solid weight of her hand in his, only her sweet scent in his nose.

He breathed in deeply, not realizing until she spoke that he'd let his eyes fall closed.

"What would happen if you didn't turn on the news? If you turned off your cell phone for a few hours? If you left the prince back at the castle?"

Nothing. Nothing would happen. His mother was the reigning monarch. Taking care of the country was her duty, for now and for decades to come.

Mother and Father might worry if they tried to reach him and couldn't. They'd forgive him once he turned his phone back on.

Conrad would handle anything that came up.

But—

"I'm not sure I can do it." He opened his eyes as he admitted it. He wanted to see her expressive face. "I've buried myself in my duties for so long... Apart from the prince, I'm not even sure I know who the man is."

Her eyes were soft. He wanted... he wanted things he shouldn't be thinking about.

"The man needs a shower." She said the words with an adorable wrinkle of her nose. "And then coffee. And then you can decide what to do."

Crystal was stirring pancake batter in the kitchen when she heard the shower shut off. With company watching curiously from the barstools at her counter.

She needed some way to warn Valentin what was coming.

But fatigue and confusion had her by the throat. She was out of ideas. She was going to have to bluster her way through this. She made her way around the counter but was too slow to catch the prince.

Valentin stopped short out of the hallway when he spotted the two men sitting casually on stools.

She'd raided the recesses of her closet to find the track pants that had once belonged to Michael and an oversize sweatshirt that she'd stolen from Reid last winter. She'd never seen the prince dressed so casually. It was his wary expression that she wanted to ease if she could.

And then Michael spoke. "You spent the night with the crown prince?"

Reid barked, "Is that my sweatshirt?"

She pressed the ball of her hand into the center of her forehead. It didn't relieve the pressure there, but it made her feel slightly more sane.

"It wasn't like that," she hissed at Michael. "He was ill. He slept on the sofa. I slept in my bedroom." She ignored Reid's statement and turned to Valentin, who remained frozen only a step out of the hallway. "Valentin, these two cretins are my younger brothers. Michael and Reid."

Her introduction seemed to galvanize Valentin, and he crossed the room to shake their hands.

From behind the prince's back, she gave both brothers the stink eye. They knew how to behave. She'd witnessed it before.

The question was whether they would.

"How do you know my sister?" Reid asked with the same suspicion he'd used when asking about the shirt.

"I'm working for him," she said at the same time Valentin said, "We're friends."

And then Valentin was meeting her gaze, his expression frank and more open than she'd ever seen it. "Friends."

Her heart thumped, hard, as she held his stare. After last night, she knew what it cost him to say that.

I've got a heart of stone, haven't you heard?

"Friends," she whispered. She finally broke the stare and realized both her brothers were watching them with wide, curious eyes.

Reid broke the silence first. "Uhh. You're burning the eggs."

She smacked her brother on the arm. "I haven't started the eggs." She moved around them, around the edge of the bar and back into the kitchen proper. "Valentin, I'm sorry. My brothers and I have a standing Saturday morning breakfast. I tried kicking them out, but—"

"We're bigger than she is." Michael grinned.

That. And she hadn't tried very hard. She loved her brothers, and this was usually her only chance to see them during the week thanks to busy university schedules and her own crazy job.

Valentin padded into the kitchen behind her. He was barefoot. The crown prince of Glorvaird was barefoot in her kitchen.

Eggs. She tried to get herself back on track, but it

was hard while he was so close. Her kitchen would never be described as "roomy," and having him in it made it feel downright cramped.

"I was promised coffee," he said.

"Yes. Coffee." The pot had finished percolating. She used her chin to point to the upper cabinet where she kept the mugs. "Milk's in the fridge."

"Shouldn't you pour it for him?" Michael asked with a cheeky grin. If she blinked, she could still see the ten-year-old boy he'd been sitting with legs swinging off the barstool.

"If you really work for him..." Reid said, suspicion still dripping from his voice.

"Not that kind of work." Valentin appeared completely unruffled, but she could sense the fine tension in the tightness around the edges of his smile. "Your sister is working on my love life."

Her brothers broke out into hoots and laughter.

She shifted from pouring pancake batter onto the griddle to cracking eggs into a bowl. She pretended each one was either Reid's or Michael's head and took particular satisfaction from cracking them open. "Watch it," she said. "Unless you want some arsenic with your scrambled eggs."

Valentin sent her a puzzled look.

"They're picturing me all dolled up and on your

arm at a state function," she told him, "which they apparently find hilarious."

He frowned.

"Crystal is most comfortable in sweats and a T-shirt," Michael said. "She's not exactly in the same category as the women you're used to dating."

She was whisking the eggs with vicious wrist action when Valentin moved in next to her, nudging her with his elbow as he reached for a spatula.

He flipped the pancakes easily, not even setting his coffee mug down. He was a pro.

Meanwhile, she was overheating at his nearness.

"Maybe I'm tired of women who are all style and no substance," Valentin said.

The words surprised her so much, she looked up into Valentin's face.

One of her brothers, she couldn't tell which, snorted softly. But she couldn't tear her gaze from Valentin's as he looked down at her.

"Maybe I'm looking for someone more like your sister."

At that, her brothers fell silent.

He didn't mean it, of course. Or he did, the part about wanting someone *like* Crystal. Not Crystal specifically.

Telling herself that enabled her to finally break the stare.

She poured her eggs into the skillet, where they sizzled. "I'll remember that when I'm choosing your candidate for date number three. 'Someone like me.'"

Valentin smirked, but there was something behind his eyes that she couldn't make out.

He flipped the first four pancakes onto her brother's plates, splitting them equally.

"Good plan," she said as he poured more batter onto the griddle. "Sometimes feeding them distracts the grizzly bears from their playthings."

He laughed, then turned to ask her brothers what they were studying and how their classes were and when they'd graduate. Not soon enough.

She needed to match Valentin or she wouldn't have the money to pay their next semester's tuition.

"And what about your parents?" he asked, including her in the question as he leaned back in the corner where her counter made a V. He now had a plate full of pancakes and eggs in hand and had abandoned his coffee mug to the counter beside him. "I'm realizing I've been remiss in knowing the things a friend should know."

"Dad died right after Reid was born," she said. "And Mom passed three years ago."

"Crystal's been our mom in every way that counts," Michael offered. "Our mom worked a lot, so Crystal was always the one fixing dinners and tucking us into bed and helping us with our homework."

"Doing our homework for us," Reid said.

She rolled her eyes. That'd been one time.

"She makes a mean pot of spaghetti and meatballs." Michael let his fork clank onto his plate, a satisfied sigh escaping him as he sat back and rubbed his stomach. "We had it almost every night for supper."

"Can't get her to do our laundry, though," Reid pouted. "Not since I turned ten."

She stuck her tongue out at him. And then caught herself, stealing a glance at Valentin. He was watching her with a bemused expression.

"So she's bossed you two around your entire lives. And then she invented a career where she gets to boss other men around in the guise of finding them a woman?"

She gaped at him.

"When you put it that way..." Michael lifted a hand over his mouth as if he were considering it.

She tossed a crumpled paper towel at the prince. "What? How dare you! I feed you breakfast and this is the thanks I get?"

He didn't even have to dodge her ineffective missile. The paper towel fell harmlessly to the floor well short of him. "Bad aim," he said cheerfully, stuffing another bite of eggs in his mouth.

"Try the saltshaker," Reid offered.

"Or your pancake," said Michael.

She went back to her breakfast. "I'm not going to make a mess that I'll just have to clean up." She smiled. "I'll just choose someone really obnoxious for your next date, princey-poo."

Valentin did not look impressed.

"Let's see. There was someone from your university days. She claimed to have been your perfect match. What was her name...? Hildy? Hilary?"

She tapped the tines of her fork against her lips.

Now Valentin was going a little green. "You wouldn't dare."

"Heidi! That was it. I happen to have her phone number in my files. I'm sure she'd love a chance to catch up."

He set his mostly empty plate on the counter. "I'll have you run out of the country," he said sternly.

"What?" Michael asked.

"She was in a couple of my early college classes and is obsessed with royalty," Valentin said. "She followed me around for weeks, constantly asking me out for coffee or drinks. There's no way—"

He broke off when her giggles escaped.

And the look he shot her was pure venom. The

benign kind, a look she'd received from her brothers frequently during their childhood.

"I am relieved to know you're only cruel enough to joke about torturing me with a date with a maniac. Not actually cruel enough to submit me to it."

"I wouldn't be so sure," Reid said before he slurped his coffee. "She's got a mean streak. Once dyed all my unmentionables pink."

"That was *Michael*," she said.

Unmentionables? Valentin mouthed to her.

She shrugged, a second case of the giggles sucking her under.

Some time after Crystal's brothers left, Valentin found himself lying flat on his back on the floor, staring up at her ceiling. There was a plaster patch in one corner, he thought. At some point, there'd been a leak there.

She'd shooed him out of the kitchen when he'd volunteered to help clean up. So he'd come in here and now listened to her rattling around as she washed up. He just basked in the sunshine.

"Who is Harry?" he called out to her.

He'd overheard Michael murmur to her as the two men had been leaving the apartment. *I like him much so much better than Harry.*

And for some reason, he felt a burning need to know who Harry was. A friend? An ex-husband?

He heard the tinking of dishes. She didn't answer, and he wondered if maybe she hadn't heard.

And then she did answer, hesitatingly. "Harry was my ex-boyfriend."

"Ah." What was the twisty, uncomfortable feeling in his gut? It couldn't be jealousy. He had no claim on her. They were friends.

"Are you dating anyone now?" That was a friendly thing to ask, wasn't it?

More swishing. More clinking. "No. Things didn't... end well with Harry. It's made me a little gun shy."

Join the club.

"What happened?"

She didn't answer.

"Sorry. Too personal," he called out. Though he was dying to know.

There was a clatter as if she'd dumped a bunch of silverware into her dishwasher, and then the thing started with a soft hum and glug.

"It's okay. I've pried into your personal life, haven't I?"

He caught movement from the corner of his eye, as if she was moving around the kitchen now. Wiping down the counters, maybe.

She sighed. "He wanted me to be someone I'm not. His mom didn't like my job, thought I should go to university for something else. I thought he respected what I do, but... he wanted a society wife. And I'm definitely not that."

Her brothers had joked about it during breakfast. Had their quips hurt her feelings? Or was that just normal interplay within a functional family? He'd never questioned whether his mother loved him, but the crown demanded much of her time. There was not a lot of time for teasing or horseplay within the royal family.

So what if she didn't want to give up her job to meet the expectations of some jerk's mother? That made her independent. From what he'd gathered, she was helping fund her brothers' tuition. If she'd given up her matchmaking gig, who would've helped them?

"I'll get back out there eventually," she said. "I've just been... busy."

The truth or an excuse? He didn't know.

At least she was courageous enough to try again. Not like him. He was determined to stay out of the game. He'd agreed to give her four dates, but he didn't plan on falling in love.

No thanks.

She appeared in his field of vision, looking down at him. Time to go?

"Do you need me to leave?" he asked. "I can call Conrad." He made the offer but it was halfhearted.

"You can stay, your orneriness. How are you feeling?"

"Like I want to lie on your floor forever."

She frowned as she bent to touch his temple with the back of her wrist. "At least your fever hasn't come back."

And then she surprised him by lying down on the couch beside him, also looking up at the ceiling. He supposed there wasn't enough floorspace for them both down here.

Although it might've been cozy to try.

She was only silent for a few seconds. "I don't think you'd really be content to hide here for longer than a day. I'm quite a boring person, even with my job bossing people around."

He smiled. He'd been proud of that crack earlier, and her brothers had found it hilarious.

"I like your brothers," he said. "It's obvious they adore you."

"They adore free meals once a week." But he heard the affection in her voice.

"Do you want to know my most vivid memory of my brother? Not this last mess," he hastily clarified.

She murmured a soft assent.

"I had my fourteenth birthday party. I thought I'd grown past kiddie parties, but Max insisted we let the castle staff put on an event on the castle grounds and invite our friends from school. I was convinced no one would come. I had a hard time making friends in school." He hadn't intended to share that part. "About twenty kids came. A mix of kids from my class and Max's. We played cricket and ate cake until our stomachs ached."

"It sounds like fun," she said softly.

"It was. All the way until the party was breaking up and I discovered my brother handing hundred dollar bills to each guest. He'd paid everyone to come."

Mother had been furious. For a while, Max had insisted he'd done it as a way to help his brother. But after he was pushed, Max had admitted—

"He thought of me as dull, and he'd wanted a chance to punish me for being... I think he put it 'perfectly boring'."

Her arm slipped off the edge of the couch. He didn't think anything of it until her hand clasped his on the floor.

She didn't say anything as he let himself relive the humiliation of that day. Not only the embarrassment in front of the people he'd hoped were his friends, but how devastated he'd been to discover what Max really thought of him. He and his brother had been the best of friends as small children and throughout grade school. They'd never recovered from that one event.

"Family can be cruel." He heard her quiet words but was more focused on the sensation of her skin against his as she threaded their fingers together.

He'd called her his friend today, but that title didn't feel quite right. Not anymore.

"Don't think you can distract me," she said after a few minutes of silence had passed. "You wouldn't be happy hiding here, and we both know it."

He grunted. She might be right, but he wasn't admitting to it.

"You're a good man," she said. "A man who loves his people too much to leave them without your leadership."

He scowled. "Do you have to be so reasonable?"

Her thumb rubbed a slow line against the fleshy part of his palm. "That is not one of the usual flaws I'm accused of."

Of course he was going to turn his phone on. Return to the castle.

Couldn't he enjoy these last few moments with a beautiful woman and pretend like he hadn't any cares in the world?

He'd even face off with his brother.

"What?" she asked.

"Hmm?"

"You sighed. What were you thinking about?"

He let go of her hand, throwing his wrist over his eyes. "Why did he have to come back?"

She made to response, but he could hear her reasonable response in his head. *He said he needs help.*

"I can't trust him," he muttered. "Why should I let him back into my life just because he claims he's sorry?"

When she still didn't speak, he moved his arm so he could see her. "That wasn't a rhetorical question."

She rolled over onto her stomach and propped her chin on her hands so that she was looking at him. "Who can you trust?"

He considered that for a moment. "My father."

"Why don't you let your father talk to Max first and then trust his judgment?"

"I'd feel like my mother, using Father as a go-between."

She raised that expressive brow and he explained. "My father is more sensitive to relationship issues."

Her lips twitched in a smile. "So you're your mother's son?"

Any humor he'd felt at the mention of his father turned into a scowl. "Probably."

She reached out and patted his shoulder. "This is helpful."

He couldn't see it. "How so?"

"Oh, not to you." Her gaze had gone far-off, as if she was thinking furiously. "To me. Your perfect match is someone who can finesse difficult relation-ships, see the connections, ease tense situations. I'm sure I know someone like that."

He was beginning to think he did, too.

Chapter Six

Just turn it off.

But Crystal was frozen on her sofa, her eyes glued to the cricket match on the television.

She'd meant to turn it on in the background as she folded and ironed her laundry, but her clothes were still in the hamper next to her feet on the coffee table.

Because the camera kept panning to Valentin and Pansy sitting close together in the stands, watching the match. He'd made good on his promise to connect with her again after the aborted coffee date.

And Crystal felt sick to her stomach as she watched the interplay between the two.

Leaning close enough that their shoulders touched as they spoke to each other.

Laughing together.

Unlike his date for the state dinner, it was clear to anyone with eyes that there was a connection between them.

The coverage cut to a commercial, and she blindly reached for the remote, turning off the telly completely.

But she didn't get up, didn't fold clothes.

This was good. She'd known Pansy would be a match for Valentin. Pansy was beautiful and sensitive and successful.

This was what she'd wanted. How many matchmakers could say they'd made a royal match? With a few whispers in the right ears, she'd have so much business she wouldn't be able to keep up.

So why did she feel like this was wrong?

She swiped at an errant tear. Stupid.

She stood, but only to throw a punch at the nearest throw pillow.

What had she really thought? That just because Valentin had let her offer him comfort that... what? He'd fall in love with *her*?

She might be successful at her job, but she didn't come from a royal lineage. Didn't have extensive connections in the political world.

She had two younger brothers whom she loved more than anything else in the world.

But she wasn't anybody special.

Her brothers had joked about it during that most recent breakfast together, but it was true. She wouldn't be able to hold her own in conversation about current events or the political climate. She wasn't a fashionista who could demand every eye be on her when she was in the public eye.

And most importantly, she wasn't in contention because she'd been hired by the crown. No matter how unconventional the royal family was—three princesses married to cowboys and a secret half-sister princess—royalty didn't marry the hired help.

She tried to think, but it was like trying to force her brain through frozen sludge.

The prince had asked for a meeting with her tomorrow. But if he'd hit it off with Pansy—and it seemed like he had—he wouldn't need her assistance anymore.

Maybe she could cancel.

Then she'd never have to see him again. Except in her dreams.

I had a great time tonight.

Valentin stared at the text message from Pansy.

The day limo had pulled in to the castle garage, but he delayed as he tried to formulate a response.

He liked Pansy, but...

His phone buzzed again. *I hope it works out for you and Crystal.*

He grimaced and typed a quick, *Thanks.*

He hadn't meant for it to happen, but it seemed like every third sentence out of his mouth had been something about Crystal. He'd wondered what she'd think of a crazy fan's war paint from head to toe. He'd mentioned how funny she'd been when she was with her brothers. He'd even let it slip how much he liked her.

Fine, so he hadn't actually *said* that one, but Pansy was intuitive enough to figure it out. And she was a good sport, happy to bow out in favor of her friend.

Crystal had chosen wisely. If he wasn't already enamored with her, he'd have gotten along well with Pansy.

He followed his bodyguard through the garage and found his father waiting for him just inside.

"We need to talk," Father said, "if you've got the time."

That sounded serious, and his stomach plunged. He'd spoken to his father briefly about Max.

"Always have time for you."

They walked together to the first-floor parlor that was decorated in tones of maroon and gold.

"I suppose this is about Max." Valentin forced himself to release the tension that had taken residence in his shoulders. He propped his hands on the stone windowsill and leaned back on them.

"Tell me."

"Annika passed."

The news hit him like a physical blow. He exhaled the shock.

"How?"

"A car accident. A few days after the baby was born."

The baby. Max had a baby. Max was a single father. No doubt he wanted help. His brother hadn't been able to keep a pet fish alive for more than a few days, and now he was a *single father?* Being on his own must have been a world different from living in the palace with a staff to support him.

"Did you know? You and Mother? About the pregnancy."

Father nodded. "Your mother hired private investigators when he left. She's gotten weekly reports. And I've spoken to him on the phone a few times. I didn't think you'd want to know."

Valentin nodded. Father was right. He'd wanted ignorance.

"What does he want?" Other than a piece of Valentin's soul. Just imagining Max moving back into the palace made him want to throw something. And if he brought Annika's daughter? The daughter Valentin had imagined would be his own...?

His chest was tight as if he might be suffering a panic attack. He fought for breath.

"He wants to talk to you. To apologize."

He shook his head. "I don't think so." Tonight, he'd been lost in thoughts of Crystal. How long had it been since he'd been mired in memories of Max and Annika together? Even that morning at her apartment, being with Crystal had muted the pain.

Now the pain was back with blinding intensity.

He shook his head again. "I can't."

Father clasped his hand on Valentin's shoulder. "Easy, son. Easy."

He exhaled a shaky breath. He didn't like being this vulnerable. Didn't want his father—or anyone—to see him like this.

But he was safe with Father. He knew that.

"I stopped loving her the moment she betrayed me. But Max—"

"He's still your brother."

How could he have done it to Valentin? How could Max hate him so much? What had Valentin ever done to him?

There weren't good answers for any of Valentin's questions. Even if he met with Max, he doubted he'd get answers that would heal the rift between them.

"You don't have to decide tonight," Father said.

Valentin took several more breaths to steady himself before he broke away.

"How was your date? Things with the matchmaker working out?"

Valentin laughed, but there was a bit of hysteria in it. "The date was passable. Crystal is..."

"More than passable, I guess?" Father asked when Valentin trailed off.

"Amazing. Intuitive. Caring. I think I'm falling for her. I thought I was..."

He pressed both palms against his eye sockets.

"How can I be falling for her if I'm still so messed up over what Max did to me?"

Father sighed. "You pulled away from everybody after what happened. You've been coming back to life these past few weeks. I'm guessing it's because of her."

Coming back to life. Like a limb that had been cut off from blood flow and lost circulation. Now life-giving blood was rushing back through each blood vessel. And it was painful. Doubly so with the wound Max had left still open and bleeding.

"I don't know what to do, Dad" he admitted. The term slipped out.

Father straightened infinitesimally. "Been a long time since you called me that. Or asked me for advice."

Had it? He'd been an arrogant fool up until things had happened with Annika and Max, and then his world had gone into a tailspin.

Dad smiled at him. "You remind me of your mother when we first met. She'd put up these walls to keep everyone out."

So had he. He'd done it gleefully, been happy to have an excuse not to put himself out there again. So he couldn't get hurt.

But he'd been withering away inside. Dying slowly without real companionship.

Until Crystal had obliterated his walls with that very first meeting.

"You want my advice?" Dad asked. "Here it is. You grab hold of that girl and don't let go."

Chapter Seven

As Crystal walked in to the palace her stomach threatened to revolt. She should've tried harder to cancel the meeting with Valentin.

When she'd texted him first thing that morning saying that something had come up, he'd responded with, *I need to see you.*

And when she'd still been chewing on how to respond to that, still telling her leaping heart to settle down, that he didn't mean it like that, he'd texted again. *Your presence is required at the agreed upon time.*

How was it possible that his pompous tone could come through in a text message? She didn't know, but hearing it had obliterated all of her softer feelings, clouded them with anger at his high-handedness.

She was clinging to that anger now, purely as a matter of survival. Following Conrad through the winding passageways meant she was getting closer and closer to the moment when Valentin would break her heart.

And then the assistant was knocking softly on a door—not Valentin's suite this time—and opening it to usher her inside.

It was a lovely, well-appointed parlor in creams and blush tones.

The romantic atmosphere of the room only served to heighten her discomfort. And then there was Valentin, rising from where he leaned against the arm of a massive brocade sofa.

He wore dark slacks and a white shirt that had been left open at the collar, as if he'd discarded his tie. His sleeves were rolled up, revealing the corded muscles of his forearms.

It was more casual than she'd seen him dressed anytime other than that morning in her apartment.

She didn't dare think about that morning right now.

"You came." He sounded... relieved? He stepped toward her, because she hadn't moved once Conrad had practically pushed her in the doorway and closed the door behind her.

"I almost didn't. I don't like being ordered around."

One corner of his mouth twitched. Not really a smile, but a hint of one.

He took another step toward her. "I've missed you these past few days."

That was... not what she expected him to say. He was supposed to tell her he'd fallen for Pansy. She was supposed to congratulate him.

But his statement had put them off the script, and she didn't know what to say in response.

There was no way she was admitting to the insane jealousy she'd experienced last night.

"The date last night went well, didn't it?" she asked stiffly.

He waved her question away. "It was fine."

Fine. It had looked more than fine in the snatches she'd seen.

"So you'll be seeing her again?" she confirmed. She needed to get out of there.

"No."

He'd come a step closer somehow and now stood at the boundary of her personal space. He filled up her vision, but she tried to look beyond him as her emotions surged in crazy directions.

She cleared her throat. "Do you want me to find someone else for the fourth date?"

The little girl inside her, the one who'd once dreamed of being a princess, was screaming *no!* even as she fought for composure. She wasn't sure she could do it, not with the feelings she harbored for Valentin. The crush that had exploded out of proportion like a stalk grown from magic beans.

Her emotions were totally out of bounds.

And then he took one more step. Into her space. Got so terribly and wonderfully close that she could smell his spicy shampoo, could see the shadow of scruff at his jaw that must have meant he hadn't shaved that morning.

He put his hands on her waist, and she froze.

"I want the fourth date, and all the dates after that, to be with you."

She'd dreamed of him saying something that crazy.

But she'd never been able to finish those daydreams. Because she was just Crystal. She'd never been able to picture the reality of how she might fit into his life.

And now that he was standing close, touching her, saying romantic words, fear rose up to choke her. She *didn't* fit in his life.

He squeezed her waist lightly. "Crystal. Tell me I'm not alone in my feelings."

It was the vulnerability behind his gruff demand that made her respond. She nodded. Then shook her head. She couldn't think.

And then he made it even more impossible when he leaned forward and bent his head.

How could she resist him?

How could she not rise up on her toes and meet his kiss?

She wanted his kiss, needed it.

Her hands came to his shoulders. To steady herself, that was all. But then she was wrapping her arms around his neck as he pulled her in closer. Her fingers weaved into the soft hair at his nape.

He groaned against her mouth, his kiss becoming deeper, more passionate. She met each one of his kisses fiercely. Because this wasn't real.

She was dreaming. That was the only explanation for what was happening. She'd fallen asleep behind the wheel and any second she was going to crash back into reality.

Valentin broke the kiss but didn't let her go as he kissed her cheek, her jaw, her temple. He was breathing hard, his chest rising and falling against hers.

This was crazy. This was—

And then reality sent her crashing back to earth.

"Val—"

The door opened.

Crystal hadn't come very far into the room, and she felt the rush of air around her.

More than that, she felt the change in Valentin. Beneath her hands, the muscles in his neck went tight.

The interruption was almost like the car crash she'd anticipated. The bone-jarring thud of running into something stationary, a hit that rattled her bones.

Max stood in the doorway wearing a look of utter surprise.

She was shaking as she tried to extricate herself from Valentin's embrace. It wasn't hard when he set her away.

What was Max doing here? She didn't think he'd been allowed in the palace since he'd broken Valentin's heart.

"I'll go," she said, but Valentin had her hand in a vice grip.

"Stay, please."

She was unmoored, out to sea without a life raft. So she let herself be carried further into the room, let Valentin pull her to the sofa, then urge her down next to him. They were sitting so close that their thighs were pressed together.

Max joined them, his gaze sharp and curious and at the same time, repentant.

What was going on?

Valentin's heart was racing. His emotions were a tangled mess. And he couldn't seem to let go of Crystal's hand as he stared at his brother across the low table.

He'd meant to talk to Crystal. Tell her everything that was in his heart and ask her not to abandon him.

But he'd kissed her instead. Because that was easier than explaining the emotions shredding him from the inside.

And now he had to deal with Max. His brother had always been perpetually late. Of course today would be the day he chose to be early. Valentin had wanted things settled with Crystal before he'd had to face his brother. She was by his side, letting him cling to her like a little kid, but nothing was resolved between them.

Max looked different. Fatigue lined his eyes, and there was a softness there that Valentin didn't recognize. Had it been there on the street last week and he'd been too angry and too ill to see it?

And then there was the fact that as Max settled in the chair across from them, he was glancing between Valentin and Crystal with undisguised curiosity. Everything between them was still new, and a fierce protective urge rose up in him. He didn't even want his brother to see the tenuous threads holding them together.

"Thanks for meeting with me," Max said when it was clear Valentin had nothing to say. He shifted in his seat, looking more uncomfortable than Valentin had ever seen him. "I... I'm sorry."

Max had said it on the street. And now for the second time. Before this, he couldn't remember ever hearing his brother say the words.

And he seemed sincere, which was even more shocking.

"I know I can't repair our relationship. I don't deserve your forgiveness, but..." Max sighed. "I have to try. Clara deserves to know her family."

Valentin bristled. But Crystal squeezed his hand, a momentary distraction.

Max's gaze met his, but his eyes quickly darted away. "She even deserves to know her uncle, a much better man than her father."

All the breath caught in his chest. Valentin

didn't know what to say, and when another of Max's glances caught what must have been the stunned expression on Valentin's face, Max laughed bitterly.

"You never knew, did you?" Max ran a hand through his hair. "I was always jealous of you. From the moment I started toddling around after you."

"You called me dull. Said I was a slave—"

"—to your duty. I remember." Max winced. "You made it seem so easy. You genuinely wanted your destiny. You and Mother were close because of it. And in Father's eyes, you could do no wrong. I wanted to be you."

Valentin shook his head. No. That was not how he remembered it.

"Is that why—?" He choked on the words.

"Is that why I romanced Annika?" Max looked down at the floor. Was this the true test, then? If he was really repentant, Valentin would find out now.

And for a long moment, it seemed his brother wouldn't answer.

Crystal nudged his knee with hers. "Are you sure you want to know?" she asked softly.

Did he want to know?

He glanced at the woman beside him, met her gaze squarely. He was a little surprised she hadn't run from the room. This wasn't her battle. Yet she'd stayed.

He wasn't just falling for her. He'd fallen. He'd dived off the deep end. He was in love with her.

Knowing why Annika had betrayed him didn't matter. He knew, deep in his heart, that Crystal would never do such a thing.

But maybe knowing what had been the root of Max's actions would help as he tried to navigate the difficult relationship with his brother.

"Tell me," he said, looking back to Max.

Max hadn't missed the interplay between them. Thankfully, he didn't comment on it. "At first, it was pure jealousy. I thought to flirt with her and make your relationship more difficult. I didn't even know if it was possible. But the more stolen moments I spent with her..." He exhaled softly, and there were real tears standing in his eyes. "I fell in love with her. I knew it was wrong. I should've come to you. But things spiraled out of control, and then it was too late. And I let my pride and arrogance and jealousy ruin what relationship we had left."

Valentin doubted he would've understood even if Max had tried to confess to him. He had his own pride, and it would've been deeply wounded no matter what.

They sat there, Max beseeching him in silent entreaty while Valentin tried to come to terms with it all.

Would he have really been happy with Annika? He would never know. But he did know that if he'd still been with Annika, he never would've met Crystal. Everything that had happened had brought him to this moment.

Max stood with a frustrated exhale. "I won't ask for your forgiveness—"

"Well, that's just stupid," Crystal burst out.

She gasped softly and let go of Valentin to press her fingers against her lips. She looked chagrined, a faint blush staining her cheeks.

Max had stilled, a picture of wary curiosity.

"Go ahead," Valentin said. "Put us in our places."

She shook her head, still pressing her hand against her mouth. "I'm sorry. I shouldn't have..." she mumbled behind her fingers.

Max laughed. Actually laughed, a rusty chuckle. "I like her," he said to Valentin. Then, "Please, go on."

Crystal's blush was rosier now, filling her whole face, but she dropped her hand. "If it's forgiveness you want, why wouldn't you ask for it?" she said. "Pride? Or stubbornness?" She looked between them. "It seems like you've both got more than enough of both."

Valentin smiled grimly. She was not wrong.

She was focused on Max. "Maybe you'll be denied what you want. Or maybe the answer will be 'not yet.' But if you don't ask, you're only punishing yourself."

Max looked from Crystal to Valentin. All signs of humor had vanished from his expression. If anything, he looked as grim as Valentin felt. And Valentin could see the moment when he braced himself, a minute straightening of his shoulders.

"Val. I've wronged you, and I'm sorry. Can you ever forgive me?"

Valentin stood.

And Max straightened his shoulders again, as if he was bracing for a punch.

There were so many things he could hold against his brother, so many reason to hang onto his anger, his resentment, his hate. But none of those things had done Valentin a bit of good. They'd only made him angry and bitter.

Max's betrayal had wounded him. Withholding forgiveness would only would him more. He glanced at Crystal, who seemed to be holding her breath beside him. Bitterness would add jagged edges all of his relationships.

And he wanted nothing but softness between himself and Crystal.

And deep in his heart, he wanted Max back. "I forgive you. Brother."

Max exhaled a long breath.

Valentin stuck out his hand. Maybe a handshake was too impersonal, but he couldn't offer a hug. Not yet. But maybe one day.

Max took it, his grip sure and steady. He didn't try to squeeze or play any one-upmanship games. He met Valentin's stare with a level gaze of his own. "Thank you."

And if Max's eyes were a little wet, Valentin's were slightly misty too, so he mustn't have seen it.

Crystal watched from her perch on the couch as Max took his leave. She felt a hundred pounds lighter on Valentin's behalf that he'd been able to forgive his brother. There would still be hurdles in their relationship. Some wounds could be forgiven but not forgotten. But today they'd forged a new start.

When Valentin turned to face her, she stood. She should've already taken her leave.

Because as she'd been sitting beside Valentin, she'd realized the reason he'd kissed her, had clung to her hand when she'd tried to excuse herself.

And she felt like she was bleeding all over the carpet. All her hopes, dashed to pieces along with her heart.

She couldn't bear to look at him, so she kept her

gaze safely on the wall over his shoulder as she tried to manufacture a smile.

"I should get going."

He must've been lost in thoughts of his brother, because now she felt the sharpness of his gaze as it fixed on her. "We have things to talk about."

Her smile slipped a little. "I think we're done talking."

She stood and tried to walk past him, but she didn't make it to the door before he touched her arm.

She whirled, afraid that if she let him touch her she'd come undone. But that was a mistake, because now she was facing him.

"I want to see you again," he said. "Tonight. Or tomorrow night, if you already have plans. Every night." His charming smile just made her angrier. She wasn't a servant to be pushed around at his whims.

"You can stop pretending now."

His smile faltered, quickly replaced by a frown.

His voice was carefully even when he spoke. "What are you talking about?"

"I get it." She hated that her voice shook. "Max saw us together outside the school. And today you wanted him to see you'd moved on. You wanted him to think we were together. To prove his betrayal hadn't hurt that much."

"It wasn't like that."

"No? You didn't let him think we were a couple?"

"So what if I did? I'd like to see where things go between us."

"I'm not some pawn on your chess board," she said. This time the shake in her voice was audible. She swallowed hard. She didn't want him to see how badly he'd hurt her. "You might have plenty of women happy to be a part of your power plays, but I'm not one of them."

She spun toward the door again, but he stopped her with a hand on her arm, turned her to face him again. "Hang on a minute."

A muscle was jumping in his cheek. He was really angry, though he was trying to control it. "Why exactly do you think I kissed you?"

"So I would look at you adoringly while you met with your brother."

"Do you adore me?"

Behind the frustration in his gaze, there was something else. Something that looked like vulnerability.

She couldn't answer him. Wouldn't. He was asking too much.

His chest rose and fell on a breath. "Is that really what you think of me? That I'm so mercenary I would kiss you, play with your emotions, to further my own ends?"

No. She didn't really think that of him. She buried her face in her hands. "I don't know."

Since she'd walked into the castle this morning, she'd been on an emotional roller coaster. Believing Valentin was falling for Pansy. Wanting him for her own. The elation of having him. And then realizing that he was using her to strengthen himself against Max.

What was real?

He touched her wrists. Gently dislodged her hands from her face. As she let her hands drop, his arms fell to his sides.

Tears were close to the surface. She could see that he was holding back his emotion as well. The stiffness of his stance, the careful blank expression on his face.

"Let me be clear," he said. "I am falling in love with you. That's the reason I kissed you. And I wanted you by my side during a difficult conversation with my brother because you bring me peace. Not because you're available or I want to show him up. Because I need you near me."

It was perfectly romantic and exactly the right thing to say.

And entirely too much. Her fragile emotions

couldn't handle a declaration like that, not after everything else.

"Valentin, I can't do this right now. I'm sorry."

This time when she ran for the door, he didn't stop her.

Chapter Eight

Crystal was still in bed when she heard pounding on her front door.

She answered it with bleary, tear-blurred eyes to find both of her brothers on her stoop even though it was still dark.

"What are you doing here?"

"We came to find out what's wrong," Michael said.

Reid stepped into her apartment and closed his arms around her in a hug. "You've never canceled Saturday morning breakfast before."

"We knew it must be something big." Michael followed his brother into her apartment and closed the door behind him.

How sweet. And unnecessary. She'd prefer to

still be in bed, hiding under the covers with her pillow over her head.

She tried to smile. "I didn't think you'd see my text until later. I can't believe you guys are even up this early."

"Stop trying to distract us," said Michael. "What's going on?"

She brushed a stray tear from her cheek, made her way into the kitchen, and started a pot of coffee. If she was going to have to deal with these two louts in her fragile emotional state, she needed sustenance.

"What did Princey-Poo do?" Reid asked.

She laughed, but there was a definite air of hysteria to it. "No, it's me. All me."

"I knew we should've pummeled that guy." Michael punched one meaty fist into his open palm.

"He said... he said he's falling in love with me." Even as she said the words, tears streamed down her cheeks.

Her brothers stood there dumbfounded, staring at her with their mouths hanging open.

"I will never understand women," Michael muttered.

Reid ignored his brother. "Why is this a bad thing? I thought you liked the guy."

"I do!" She tore a paper towel off the roll and dabbed at her face.

Now her brothers glanced at each other. Michael shot a look at the door, like maybe he was rethinking being in her apartment at all.

Reid wiped both hands down his face. Then he put his hands on his hips. "So he's in love with you, and you like him. I don't see what the problem is."

"We'd never fit. You said it yourself. I'm not the right woman for him."

"Uhh..." Michael was looking at her as if she were crazy.

"What are you talking about?" Now Reid was starting to sound angry. "You're the best person I know."

She sniffled. For all the grief they gave her, her brothers really were good guys.

"I'm not a... a supermodel. I can barely dress myself. I don't know anything about politics. I can't date the crown prince."

"Do you really think any of that matters to him? If he's got any brains at all, he'd be snatching you up right now and never letting you go."

She hiccupped. Dabbed her face when more tears came.

"He's right," Michael said. "The guy would be a dummy not to want you." He crossed his arms.

"You're always bossing us around. And most of the time"—he rubbed his side where Reid had thrown an elbow—"Okay, all the time you're right. But you're not telling yourself the truth right now."

Reid butted in. "You've got it in your head that you're not good enough for him, but you're a hundred percent wrong. Stupid Harry and his mother weren't good enough for you. You've still got their lies inside you. And you're believing them."

She listened to her brothers sing her praises for another few minutes before she kicked them out.

They were sweet. But wrong.

Weren't they?

She cleaned up the detritus of the coffee she'd shared with her brothers, her brain awhirl.

She wasn't good for Valentin. If she'd filled out a questionnaire or gone through one of her client interviews, she would never match herself with Valentin.

But did that mean they couldn't belong together?

She was trying to protect herself from the heartbreak that would inevitably come when he finally figured out she wasn't the one for him.

But what if rejecting him was wrong?

As crazy as it sounded, what if her brothers were right? What if she and Valentin belonged together?

. . .

Valentin pushed himself during his morning run.

Faster. Faster. Harder. Harder. Further. Further.

Until his muscles were aching and he was gasping for air.

He slowed. Jogged.

And then dropped to his knees the sand. The physical exertion wasn't helping the chaos in his head.

He couldn't outrun what was chasing him.

Crystal didn't love him.

Somehow it was worse than when Annika had betrayed him. Because he'd laid himself bare for Crystal. Made himself open, vulnerable. He'd shared parts of himself with her that he'd never revealed to Annika. Maybe it wasn't such a surprise that Annika had turned to his brother after all. Not when he'd kept part of himself safe, protected from her.

He hadn't protected himself from Crystal. He'd shown her all of himself. The darkest parts inside him, the broken pieces that had been left after Max and Annika had obliterated his heart. He'd offered her himself, just as he was.

And she'd walked away.

He sat on the beach, waiting for his bodyguard to catch up, and stared at the water, at the sun as it slowly rose over the horizon. First a sliver of light and then more.

He'd never claimed to be perfect. Only to love her.

And that wasn't enough.

He wasn't enough.

He felt desolate. Empty. More so even than when his life had imploded before.

He'd thought he had everything figured out. He'd foolishly thought that Crystal would be delighted by his declaration. Instead, she'd run away. He'd tried to call her twice later in the evening. She hadn't picked up.

He was nothing without her.

The thought settled. *Nothing without her.*

He played it over and over in his head.

And then he rejected it.

Crystal and Max had both said separately that he put duty above all else.

He was the monarch. The future king. He would always be that, Crystal or no Crystal. Future wife or no wife.

That truth settled deep inside him. He might be broken, might not have gotten the prize that he wanted, but he was whole enough to rule Glorvaird. To put his people's needs ahead of his own.

And for now, that would have to be enough.

. . .

An hour after her brothers left, Crystal was a little surprised the castle guards let her drive onto the grounds. No one stopped her when she parked near the garage.

The sun was barely up. This early, she'd probably find Valentin on his morning run. At least she hoped so. It would give her the privacy that she dearly wanted.

She rounded the castle, letting one hand trail behind her, fingertips touching the cool stone.

He was out there, his bodyguard slightly behind. He wasn't running. He was walking slowly up the beach toward the castle, his bodyguard trailing him.

Valentin was still a good distance away when the bodyguard said something to him. His head came up, and he looked at her.

Stupid bodyguard and his attentiveness to his surroundings.

She hung back by the corner of the castle wall.

She'd come this far, but she didn't know what she was going to say.

Valentin could've sent the bodyguard to send her away, but it was the prince himself who came to meet her. His T-shirt was soaked with sweat. How long had he been out here?

He hadn't shaved yet, and his hair was rumpled.

He'd never been more beautiful.

He stopped just out of arms' reach. "What are you doing here?"

She couldn't read his expression. He was unsmiling, his shoulders stiff.

She'd hurt him badly. What if he didn't want to give her a second chance?

Her lips wobbled. She tried to push down her emotion. She didn't want to cry all over him. But she couldn't hold it back.

So she whispered. "Valentin, I tried so hard not to fall in love with you. But I couldn't help it."

Hot tears stung her eyes, and she tried to hide her face. But his arms wrapped around her, pulled her close. "Oh, thank God."

He held her as she half-cried, half-laughed into his shoulder. He pressed a kiss into the hair above her ear.

"I'm sorry about yesterday," he said. "I shouldn't have pushed. I can try not to be so demanding, but I'm a work in progress."

She leaned back and wiped her tears. "It wasn't that."

He was watching her with such tender concern that it made it easier to say. "I'm more down-to-earth than your other matches. I'm no supermodel."

His hand came up to cup her cheek. He hadn't laughed at her fears or dismissed them outright. "I only want you. I love you."

She lowered her gaze. "And... I've worked hard to get where I am. I still have to get my brothers through university. How will it look that I've snagged the most eligible of all my clients?"

His thumb brushed her cheek. When she looked back into his dear face, one corner of his mouth was turned up. "I hadn't even thought about that. Not very considerate." His eyes went unfocused for a moment as he stared off into space. Then, "Conrad will write up a press release from my office."

She gulped. That sounded very official. "What will it say?"

"The truth is usually the easiest. That I simply couldn't resist your charms and you're off the dating market, but that you're still taking on new clients. Selectively," he murmured. "Not too many that you don't have time for me."

"Was that a complaint? Already?"

He grinned incorrigibly. "Conrad could also make a few discreet inquiries. I'm sure there must be some count or dignitary in my acquaintance who is looking for his match."

He'd do that for her?

She'd thought all her tears were spent, but new heat pricked her eyes.

When he leaned in and captured her lips, she raised one hand to clasp his wrist. She met his kiss eagerly.

She was safe here in his arms.

He broke the kiss and brushed her temple with his lips. "I'm getting you all sweaty."

"I don't mind," she replied dreamily.

"Come up and have breakfast with me?"

She agreed and he laced their fingers together as they walked.

She'd first come to the palace to make a match for her prince. She'd just never imagined it would be her.

Epilogue

Edward Bisson had chased down numerous stories in his career as a reporter. He'd exposed secrets and scandals. During the last two years, he'd been working for the American media as a foreign correspondent in the Middle East. He'd faced down bullets and once nearly been blown up by an IED.

So his current assignment should be a breeze. Go undercover as a cowboy. Work on a ranch while he tried to get close to a European princess and then expose her.

But this assignment might just be the most important he'd ever done.

Because Princess Tirith of Glorvaird had ruined his brother's life. She'd nearly killed his niece. Peyton had recovered partially, but the brain damage she'd suffered meant the bright little girl she'd once been would never be the same. The royal family might've footed all the medical bills, but his brother was a single father who now had to devote his whole life to taking care of Peyton.

And the princess had never faced one iota of punishment for what she'd done. Because the royal family had kept things so hush hush.

Even Edward hadn't known about her involvement in Peyton's accident until he'd accidentally uncovered some paperwork in his brother's messy office. There'd been a nondisclosure agreement signed by his brother. Carrick couldn't say anything to anyone—even his own brother—or the palace would pull funding for Peyton's ongoing care.

So Edward wasn't supposed to know about the accident or the cover-up. But that hadn't stopped him from snooping through the other paperwork in his brother's office. He'd managed to get some information from an aide at the hospital where Peyton had been treated.

Apparently, the princess had visited once or twice—as if that made up for what she'd done to his family.

Edward was angry. Furious that this had happened and that she hadn't paid.

Someone like her, someone who could damage a family and walk away scot-free, without a care in the world, deserved to pay. Someone like her had to have more dirt in the past. All he had to do was find it. Expose it.

Thus, the undercover assignment he'd given himself.

He sat on a dusty road outside some podunk town in Texas, gearing up for his entrance. Humble cowboy, down on his luck. Needed a job.

The princess was here for an extended visit with her father and to make some appearances for the family's charitable foundation. The public schedule on the royal family's website said she'd be here for six weeks.

This was his chance. Six weeks was plenty of time for revenge.

* * *

Thank you for reading THE PRINCE'S MATCHMAKER. Find out what happens when Edward comes face to face with Tirith in THE TRUE PRINCESS:

Princess Tirith of Glorvaird has supported countless charity events as a royal. But it's the charity rodeo her sister organizes that frightens her. She needs to re-learn how to ride. And she needs to do it without anyone on the Texas side of her family discovering just how deep her childhood fear of horses runs.

Tirith enlists the help of ranch hand Edward, but nothing is as it seems. The man confounds her and charms her in equal measures. He sees the woman behind the crown. When the truth of Edward's identity is revealed, Tirith realizes she's shared far too much of herself with a man who has the power to ruin her...

Also by Lacy Williams

Wagon Train Matches series (historical romance)

A Trail So Lonesome

Trail of Secrets

A Trail Untamed

Wind River Hearts series (historical romance)

Marrying Miss Marshal

Counterfeit Cowboy

Cowboy Pride

The Homesteader's Sweetheart

Courted by a Cowboy

Roping the Wrangler

Return of the Cowboy Doctor

The Wrangler's Inconvenient Wife

A Cowboy for Christmas

Her Convenient Cowboy

Her Cowboy Deputy

Catching the Cowgirl

The Cowboy's Honor

Winning the Schoolmarm

The Wrangler's Ready-Made Family

Christmas Homecoming

Heart of Gold

Sutter's Hollow series (contemporary romance)

His Small-Town Girl

Secondhand Cowboy

The Cowgirl Next Door

Cowboy Fairytales series (contemporary fairytale romance)

Once Upon a Cowboy

Cowboy Charming

The Toad Prince

The Beastly Princess

The Lost Princess

Kissing Kelsey

Courting Carrie

Stealing Sarah

Keeping Kayla

Melting Megan

The Other Princess

The Prince's Matchmaker

The True Princess

His Forever Princess

Hometown Sweethearts series (contemporary romance)

Kissed by a Cowboy

Love Letters from Cowboy

Mistletoe Cowboy

The Bull Rider

The Brother

The Prodigal

Cowgirl for Keeps

Jingle Bell Cowgirl

Heart of a Cowgirl

3 Days with a Cowboy

Prodigal Cowgirl

Soldier Under the Mistletoe

The Nanny's Christmas Wish

The Rancher's Unexpected Gift

Someone Old

Someone New

Someone Borrowed

Someone Blue (newsletter subscribers only)

Ten Dates

Next Door Santa

Always a Bridesmaid

Love Lessons

Not in a Series

Wagon Train Sweetheart (historical romance)